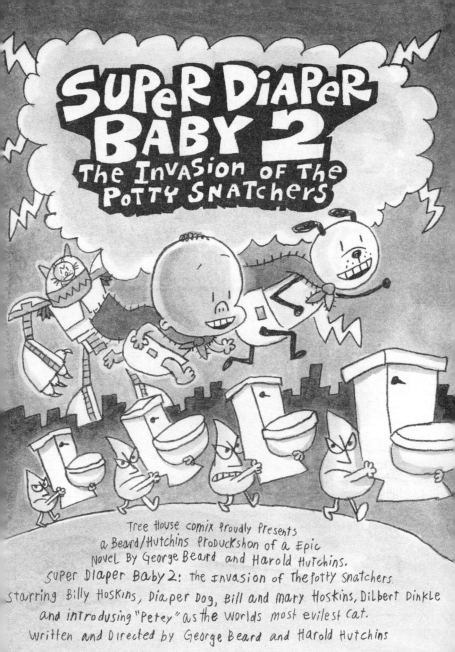

Tree House comix Proudly Presents
a Beard/Hutchins Produckshon of a Epic
Novel By George Beard and Harold Hutchins.
SUPER DIAPER BABY 2: the Invasion of The potty snatchers.
starring Billy Hoskins, Diaper Dog, Bill and mary Hoskins, Dilbert Dinkle
and introdusing "Petey" as the Worlds most evilest cat.
Written and Directed by George Beard and Harold Hutchins

this novel
has been
rated:

TA TOTALLY
AWESOME!!!
Some material may be too
Awesome for Boring old grown-ups

For Madison
Mancini

SCHOLASTIC CHILDREN'S BOOKS
AN IMPRINT OF SCHOLASTIC LTD
EUSTON HOUSE, 24 EVERSHOLT STREET
LONDON, NW1 1DB, UK
REGISTERED OFFICE: WESTFIELD ROAD, SOUTHAM, WARWICKSHIRE, CV47 0RA
SCHOLASTIC AND ASSOCIATED LOGOS ARE TRADEMARKS AND/OR
REGISTERED TRADEMARKS OF SCHOLASTIC INC.

FIRST PUBLISHED IN THE US BY SCHOLASTIC INC, 2011
FIRST PUBLISHED IN THE UK BY SCHOLASTIC LTD, 2011

ISBN 978 1407 12998 3
ISBN (C&F) 978 1407 13009 5

A CIP CATALOGUE RECORD FOR THIS BOOK IS AVAILABLE FROM THE BRITISH LIBRARY.

PRINTED IN THE UK BY CPI BOOKMARQUE, CROYDON, SURREY.
PAPERS USED BY SCHOLASTIC CHILDREN'S BOOKS ARE MADE
FROM WOOD GROWN IN SUSTAINABLE FORESTS.

1 3 5 7 9 10 8 6 4 2

WWW.SCHOLASTIC.CO.UK/ZONE

The EPic story Behind the EPic story of
Super Diaper Baby
By George B and Harold H

Once upon a while ago, there were **2** Ridonkulous kids named George and Harold.

They dont get any awesomer than us!!!

me too!

They wrote a amazing Book called the "Adventures of super Diaper Baby."

But Unforchenetly, their mean Principel, Mr Krupp read it.

It was the story of a baby who acksidentty fell into some super power juice.

splash

He drank it and got super powers and stuff.

Also, a dog drank the juice.

Glug
glug

He became super powery, too!

The baby and the dog are best friends now and they live together with their mum and dad.

They both wear diapers too!

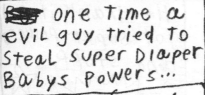
one time a evil guy tried to steal Super Diaper Babys powers...

This is going to be sweet!

Transfer Helmet

...but he made a boo-boo and got turned into poo-poo!

Hey!

Transfer Helmet

Then he got some new clear waste on him and he grew way bigger and eviler!!!

Rar!

New clear power plant

So Super Diaper Baby and Diaper Dog flew into action!

We'll get you Deputy Doo-Doo!

nuh-uh!!!

They grabbed a big Roll of toiLET paper from on top of a bilding...

BOB's TOiLET Paper compeny

HEY NO fair!

BOB

...wrapped up Deputy Doo-Doo...

...and LEFT him where all doo-doo beLongs!

WELCOM TO URANUS

Hooray for super Diaper Baby and Diaper Dog!

BUT THEN....

THIS IS GARBAGE!!!
SUPER DIAPER BABY

Its the most offensive Book I ever read!!!
SUPER DIAPER BABY
RIP

Why cant you Kids write about anything else besides PooP, huh?

scrach scrach

What else is there?
ZONG

7

Here! Read this Book!

FiLe CABiNET

Its my faverite Book from when I was a dumb kid Like you guys!

How The Grinch Stoled Christmas BY Dr. seus

Hey, how come the Last 7 pages are torn out?

Its more ReaLi-Stick that way!!!!

So George and Harold read the book and got inspired and stuff.

Hey This book is pretty good!

Yeah!

HOW the Grinch STOLeD CMAS

8

You know, I never thout Id say this, but maybe MR Krupp is right.

Maybe we **SHOULD** think about other things to write About besides Poop.

Like what?

Hmmm... Hmmm...

scrach scrach

Scrach Scrach

How About Pee?

AWESOME!!!

9

So George and Harold starded creating their all-new epic NoveL, Super Diaper Baby 2.

I bet MR KRUPP will be super happy!

me too!

They bet wrong.

What the---

SUPER DIAPER BABY 2

This is even more offensiver Than your Last Book !!!

SUPER DIAPER BABY 2

So thats The story of how Super Dia- Per Baby 2 was invented.

DETENSHON

as usual, We hope You Like It more Than Mr Krupp Did.

Bizzy Work

Bizzy Work

SUPER DIAPER BABY 2
The Invasion of the POTTY SNATCHERS

Action

Laffs

FLIP-O-RAMAS

The THIRD EPIC NOVEL BY George Beard AND HAROLD HUTCHINS

Chapters

Forwerd................. 3

1. A day at the Park... 13

2. Meanwhile............ 37

3. Daddy DiLema...... 61

4 (PART 1). Meanwhile 2 ...75

4 (PART 2). How the
   Pee Stoled Potties...... 85

5. The Aftermath........119

6. The Revenge of
   Rip Van Tinkle........151

7. Fathers Day 173

12

One day the Hoskins family went to the park for a picnick.

This looks like a nice spot.

I will set up the picnick while you boys play.

What would you like to play, Billy?

me play airplane with Daddy.

14

WARNiNG

The following flip pages start out "cuteish", but get violentish (and even violentisher) as this novel goes along.

FLiPPER'S DiSGRESHON ADViSED

FLip·O·RAMA

HEres How it works!!!!

STEP 1

PLace your Left hand inside the dotted Lines marked "LeFt Hand Here". Hold The Book open FLat.

STEP 2

GRasp the Right-hand Page with your Right thumb and index finger (inside the dotted Lines marked Right ThumB Here").

STEP 3

Now Quickly FLip The Right-hand Page back and fourth UntiL the Pitcher appears To Be Animated!

(for extra fun, try adding your own Sound Afecks).

17

FLIP-O-RAMA #1
(pages **19** and **21**)

Remember, Flip <u>only</u> page 19. While you are Flipping, be shure you can see the pitcher on page 19 <u>And</u> the one on page 21.

IF you Flip Quickly, the two pitchers will start to Look Like <u>one</u> Animated pitcher.

Dont forget to add your own Sound Afecks!

Left Hand Here

Down Goes the Airplane...

Right
Thumb
Here

Up Goes the Airplane...

FLiP-O-RAMA 2

Remember --- FLip ONLy page 23. while you are FLipping, be shure you can see the pitcher on page 23 and the one on page 25.

If you flip Quickly, The Two pitchers will start To Look Like one animated pitcher.

Dont forget Those sound afecks!

Left Hand Here

Down go the airplane

Right
Thumb
Here

up go the airplane

28

So the Hoskinses started to eat thier picknick lunch

BUT Then...

Hey mister...

Our ball got stuck up on the roof over there. Will you help us?

I shure will.

#1 Dad

#1 Dad

Wait--- my daddy got hurted!

Let super Diaper Baby handle this!

30

31

Finally the Hoskinses got BACK to finishing thier Picnick Lunch.

BUT Then...

Hey mister!

My son broke his Big Toe playing Kickball. Can you drive us To The hospitel?

I shure will!!!

Wait, Mr Hoskins. That will Take Forever!!!

I bet your still good at reading Bedtime storys!

Oh yeah!

I almost forgot. Im awesome at That!!!

Im going to go do that Right now!

#1 Dad

Oh Billy?

BILLys Room

#1 Dad

Knock Knock

Im am here to read you your faverite Bed-Time story!

Mecha-Frog and RoboToad are enemys

No daddy. me read to you Tonite!

Ha Ha! You cant read. Your Just a baby!

Actually, he can read. The super power Juice he drank also made him super smart!!! He Taught himself To read this morning!

AND SO...

..."no," shouted mecha Frog. "not unTil you deFeet my army of Ribbit Robots!".

36

This is Dr Dilbert Dinkle and his evil cat, Petey. Dr Dinkle is the one on the Left with the beard and the male-pattern Baldness. Petey is the one on the Right with the stripes and the tail.

Remember that, now!

Tonight we will rob this Bank using my new invenchon: The Liquidater 2000!

Jim's BANK

it Turns Stuff into **WATER!!!**

It does this by rearanging molecules!

and Then---

You have Bad Breath.

38

41

SPLASH

uh oh!!!

BUT THEN...

I-I got Turned into water!!!

GRRRRR

44

45

46

47

and You Know what? I Kinda Like being made out of Water!

Its Totally easy To steal stuff...

PLUS, I can hide anywhere!!!

see, Petey? I Look Just Like a puddle! You cant even see me, I bet!!!

I can still smell your Breath, Though!

So What??? I got super powers!

48

49

DRIP
DRIP
DRIP

WeLL? WHAT do you think???

seriousLy dude, you need to do something about that Breath!

WOULD YOU SHUT UP ABOUT THAT?!!?

I'm just sayin'...

And the best part about being made out of water is...

...I never have to pay my WATER Bill ever again! Think of THE SAVINGS!!!

SO ANYWAYS...

FLiP·O·RAMA 3

If you forgot how to do this already, please see your doctor. Afterwards, turn to page 17 for further instruckshons.

Left Hand Here.

Drinking Dr Dinkle

Right
Thumb
Here.

Drinking Dr Dinkle

58

60

Left Hand
Here.

Snatcher Catchers

Right Thumb Here

Snatcher Catchers

How come Daddy dont feel importent?

Im not shure... I just don't think he feels very brave or strong compared to us.

after all, we're ~~are~~ super heros and he isnt.

Help! That guy just stoled my car!!!

Haw Haw

FLIP-O-RAMA 5

Left Har Here

Jacker Smackers

Right
Thumb
Here

Jacker Smackers

Cheater Beaters!

Right
thumb
Here

Cheater Beaters!

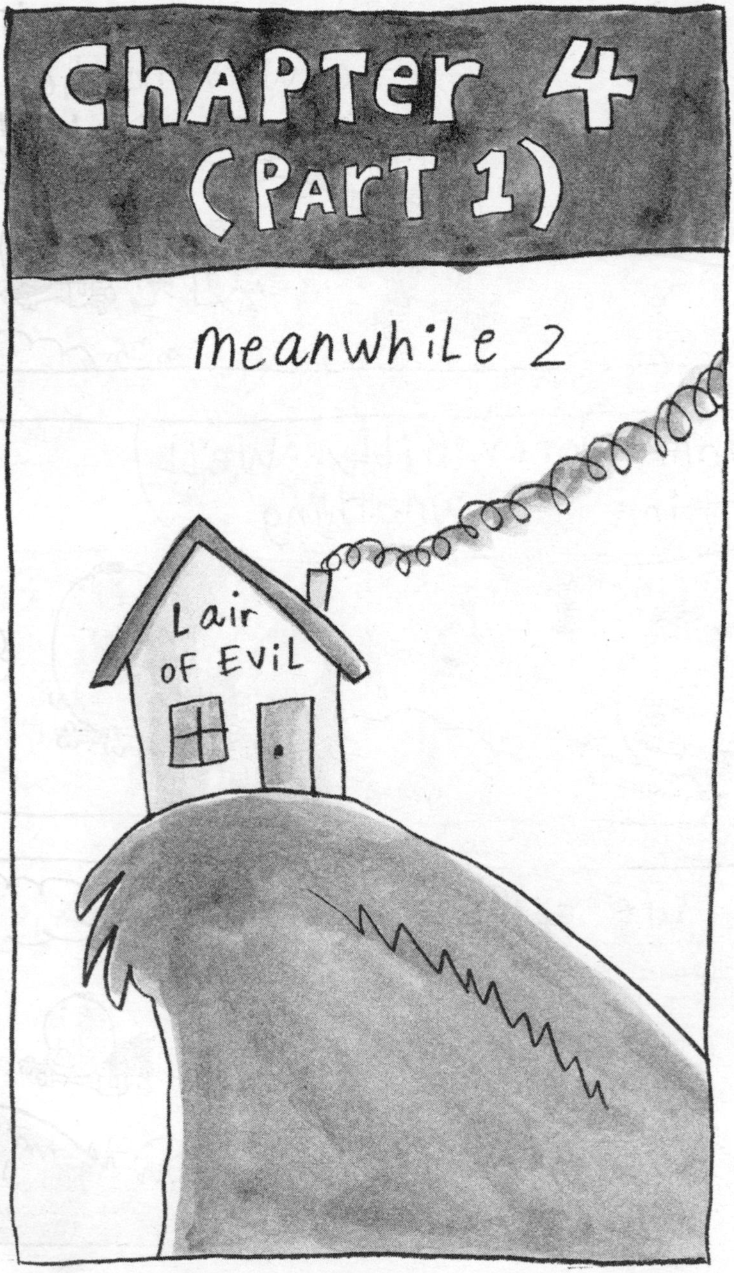
ChAPTer 4
(PArT 1)
meanwhiLe 2
Lair
OF EviL

I can't believe it! I went to sleep and when I woke up, I got turned into pee!

Hey, I should call you "Rip Van Tinkle!"

You better not!!!

Alright, Rip Van Tinkle. I won't.

YOUR in BIG TROUBLE!!!

Doncha mean "Urine" Big Trouble?

It's not funny!!! My whole body got turned into pee!!!

Hey! Maybe you'll win a Peebody Award!!!

77

78

79

83

BuT I Shall have my revenge, PeTey! Oh yes, I shall have my Revenge!!!!

I'm behind you A HUNDREDTh of PERSENT, Rip Van Tinkle!

WouLd you CuT that out?!!? Its not very nise To call PeopLe names, you Know!!!

BuT I'm one of the Bad Guys! I'm not suposed To be nise!!!

Oh yeah,

I forgot!

Tee-Hee! Being eviL RuLes!!!

84

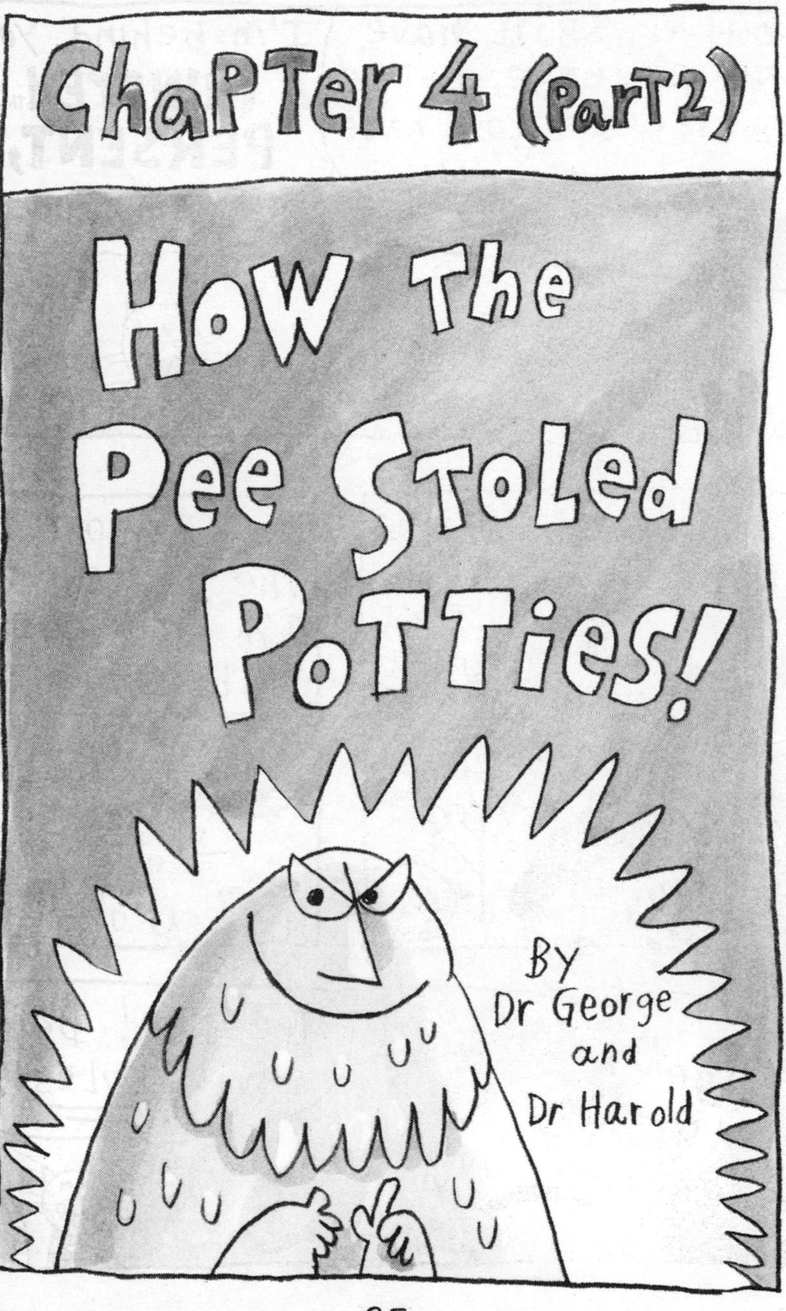
ChapTer 4 (ParT2)
How The Pee STOLed POTTies!
By Dr George and Dr Harold

That Night Rip Van Tinkle
   was frowning a frown,
as he sneered at the houses
   below in the town.

No one Knows why he was
   feeling so ruthless...
It could be because all his
   money was useless.

Or maybe because he was
just feeling cranky.
Or possibly cuz his bad breath
was so stanky.
But we think the very best
reason might be
That he smelled like a bucket
of twelve-day-old pee.

But whatever the reason
   his stank or his dough,
he stood up there hating
   the people below.
He snarled as he frowned
   feeling drearier and drearier.
"Those Jerks in the city
Think Theyr'e So Superier!

"They all be hatin´!
    But heres what I think:
 I think things would change
    if _they_ started to stink!

If all of those idiots
    smelled just like pee,
they wouldent be goin´ Round
   disrespectin´ me!!!"

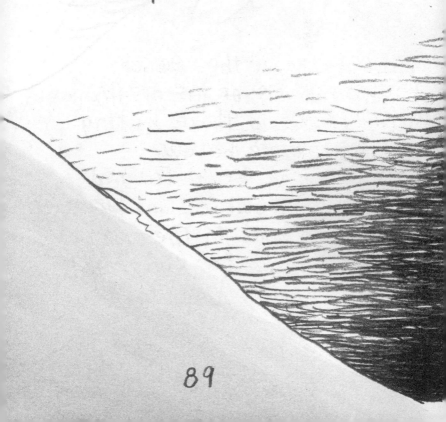

89

And then Rip Van Tinkle
   Thought up a idea.
But we couldent think up
   a rhyme for "idea".

"I know just what to do"
 he started professin'.
"I'll teach all of those good-
 smelling people a lessen!"

91

So he took some scrap metal
and used an old wheel
To build a contrapshon
with Teeth made of steel.

He hammered its tail
and sharpened its claws,
and welded its wiskers
and titened its Jaws.

It took 24 hours
From when he'd begun,
'Till the Robo-Kitty
Three Thousand was done.
"ALL I need is a driver.
I need someone mean.
I need someone evil
to run my machine".

So he took his cat "Petey"
and strapped him in tight...

...Then both of those villens sneaked out in the night.

"Watch this," Rip Van Tinkle said
Laffing out Loud...
and soon he began to
turn into a cloud.

And when the pee cloud
was over the town,
the thunderclaps crashed
and the pee drops rained down.

Into the chimneys
the pee drops they flew
And they entered each house
Knowing just what to do.

Each drop found a wrench...

... and each wrench found a bolt...

JOLT

...and soon every Toilet popped up with a JOLT!

They carried each toilet
  Right out of each house, and
Into the jaws of the
  Kitty Three thousend.

Crunch! Crunch! went the robot
without too much trouble
and soon every potty
was crushed into rubbel!

But in One Little house,
on one Little street,
One drip heard the sounds
of two Little feet.

The pee drop looked up
and what did it see?
but a cute Little tot
with a fluffy blankie.

The baby looked down
and said, "MR Pee, Hey!
Why are you taking
our toilet away?"

And that mean little drip,
do you know what it did?
why, it made up a lie
and it said to the kid:

"Your toilet is broken---
    it squeaks when you flush it.
I'LL take it away and I'LL
    clean it and brush it.

I'LL shine it right up
    -I'LL fix it and oil it,
and soon I'LL return with a
    Good-as-new toilet."

And the baby believed what
the pee drop had said.
So it got him a juice box
and took him to bed.

And at Last when the baby
was sleeping and dreaming,
that nasty old pee drop
went on with its skeeming!

He carried the toilet
Right out the door.
And once it was crushed,
He went back to get more.

The snatching of Potties
went on through the night,
And into the dawn of the
Mornings first Light.

109

And Once Every Toilet
was crushed by the cat,
The people awoke and cried,
"What up wit' dat?"

"Our toilets are gone!
We've got to go Potty!
Oh, we do not Like this!
Oh, no we do notty!"

So they each crossed their legs
and squirmed all around,
And they squeezed and they clenched,
and they bobbed up and down.

112

'Till all of the people
were doing "Pee dances"
shouting, "Someone please help us,
or we'll wet our pantses!"

They wiggled all morning
in torment and Trauma,
Just Like they're doing
in this FLip-o-Rama →

Left Hand
Here

Pee-Dance
RevoLushon

Right Thumb Here

Pee-Dance
RevoLushon

Soon, warm Liquid Streams
with Yellowish Hues
Flowed down their Legs
and filled up their Shoes.

And they sobbed as they stood
in their puddles of piddle,
But no one could help them.
Not even a Little.

Chapter 5

the Aftermath

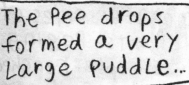

The Pee drops formed a very large puddle...

...and out of that puddle came you-know-who!

Ha! Ha! Ha!

Ho! Ho! Ho!

He! He! He! He!

Everyone Everywhere smells just like Pee!

Now they all know what its like to be me!!!

Dude, were not doing the rhyming thing Anymore.

Oh. Sorry.

So what's the next part of our evil plan?

next part?

Yeah, you know, what are we gonna do **Next**???

um... I dont know. wanna watch a movie or something?

That wasnt your **WHOLE PLAN**, was it?

What?

Are you saying we went through ALL that trouble just so people would wet their pants and smell like pee?

umm kinda

AAAAUGH!

That's the **DUMBEST** EViL PLAN I ever Heard of!

WeLL if your so smart, why dont You think up a eviL PLan!!!

OK, I WiLL!!!

Hmmm... Let me think...

NOBody has a toilet anymore...

Everybody has to go Pee-Pee...

I Got it!!!

Meanwhile at the Hoskinses House...

We've been Robed!

ALL our Toilets got Stoled, and I have to go Pee!!!

Me too!

Why don't you try on a pair of these diapers?

They work for us!

Uh... Gee, Thanks.

DiaPers

AND SO...

AAAAAAAh!

sweeeeet!!!

Hooray for Diapers!

Hi-5

124

BUT THEN .....

We interupt this show to tell you some imporant stuff!!!

5 ACTION NEWS

As you all know, everybodys toilet got stoled last night.

5 Action News

Nobody has a plase to pee anymore so the mayor has drained the city's pool...

Please feel free to pee in this empty pool until our crisis is resolved!

Local kids had this to say:

This is Awesome!

126

EXTEND
-O-TAIL

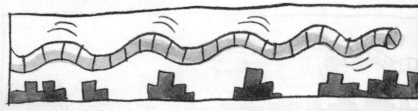

CLICK!

VRRRR!

Ka-ching!

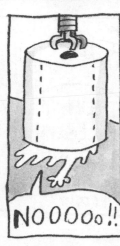

BUT There was still one Tiny drop of pee Left.

Help me!!! Please help me!

ALRight, ILL help You!

FLick

YAAAA!

I'LL Help ya Learn To FLY!!! Haw! Haw!

YAAAAAA!

Bye Bye!

YAAAAAAAAA!

133

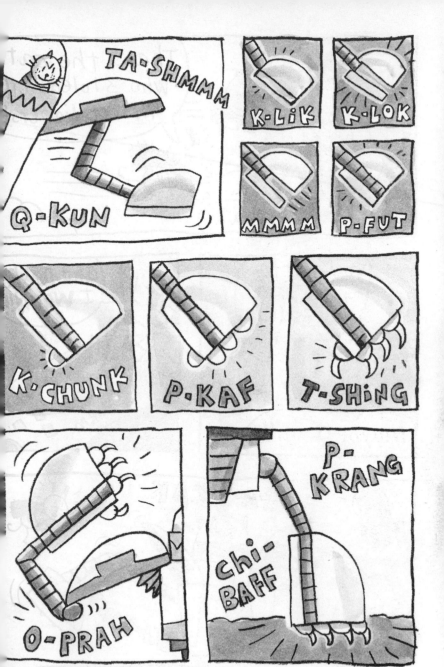

135

137

Left Hand Here

Koo-Koo For Kitty Nip!

Right
thumb
Here

Koo-Koo For Kitty Nip!

POP

FLIP-O-RAMA

Left Hand
Here

KITTY FOR KOO-KOO NIP!

KiTTY FoR KOO-KOO NiP!

CHAPTER 6

The Revenge of Rip Van Tinkle

YAAAAAA!

I Live AGAIN!

161

FLiP·O· RAMA

Left Hand Here

Building Basher

Right
thumb
Here

Building Basher

Remember back a Long Time ago when me was really Little?

You mean Last week?

Yeah!

Well, remember when me put me's Juice Box in the freezer on acksident?

Heh-Heh! Yeah, it Froze Solid!

Hey!!! Your idea just gave me a idea!!!

Push down on the ground, Billy! Push as hard as you can!!!

PUSH BiLLY, PUSH!

PUSH WITH ALL YouR MiTE!!!

BiLLy and Diaper Dog pushed and pushed...

...and slowly things began to move.

169

172

Hi mummy and Daddy!

BiLLY!

Daddy Theres a big Ice monster Outside!!!

Im so glad your safe!!!

Daddy Look at the ice monster!!

OK, OK. Lets Look at this silly ice monster of yours!

ILL Just open these curtins and take a peek!

179

Then Billy and Diaper Dog moved the Earth back to its Proper place in Space...

ZIP

...and flew back home To Join the Celebrashon!

Hey it stopped snowing!

Can I take a Pitcher of the Hero Dad for our newspaper?

OK

Hooray!!!

Left Hand Here.

Say Cheese!!!

Right
thumb
Here

say Cheese!!!

READ GEORGE AND HAROLD'S FIRST TWO EPIC ADVENTURES!

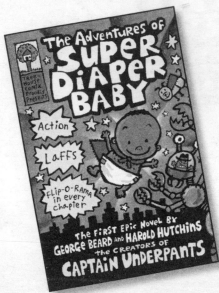

Faster than a speeding stroller, more powerful than diaper rash, and able to leap tall buildings without making poopy-stinkers, it's Super Diaper Baby!

Meet Ook and Gluk, the two coolest caveboys to step out of the Stone Age!

CAPTAIN UNDERPANTS AND the TERRIFYING RE-TURN OF TIPPY TINKLETROUSERS

Whatever happened to Professor Poopypants, that tiny tornado of terror who traumatized the people of Piqua? He changed his name to Tippy Tinkletrousers, and he has a special surprise for anybody who thinks his **NEW** name is still funny. This looks like another job for the amazing Captain Underpants!

The SUPER DiaPeR BaBY AdVeNTuRe CoNTiNueS oNLiNe AT WWW.PiLKeY.CoM AND WWW.ScHoLaSTiC.CoM

COOL!

Free Music, Video Games, Movies, and MORE!

Free!

HOW-2-DRAW PeTeY (Part 4 of 8)

HOW-2-DRAW Rip Van Tinkle (Part 3 of

HOW-2-DRAW Pee drop (side) (Part 6 of 8)

Learn to draw more than 20 characters from George and Harold's epic novels!

AWeSoMe!

MAKE YOUR OWN PeTeY
the world's most evilest Cat!

HAW! HAW!